RL 3.8

Trouble for Lucy

Lucy!" Mr. Stewart's deep voice carried above the creaking wagon wheels. "Lucy!" Get that dog away from here! How often do I have to tell you that he is not to go near the oxen."

Lucy understood why her father was so cross. Her mother was expecting a baby any day and the puppy's running and yipping only made him more touchy.

The year was 1843, and the Stewart family was emigrating to Oregon by wagon train. Before they left Independence, Missouri, Lucy's uncle had given her the puppy to keep her company on the trip. Finn was a small, frisky fox terrier who just couldn't seem to stay out of mischief.

It was bad enough trying to keep track of Finn when the wagons stopped in the big circle to make camp. But the real trouble for Lucy came one day when the wagons broke camp to move on, and Finn was nowhere to be found. Even though she knew her father would be very angry, Lucy had to sneak away from the moving wagon train and search for her puppy.

Carla Stevens' story is based on actual journals of the pioneers' journey to Oregon. The text combines with Ronald Himler's striking illustrations to bring an exciting time in American history warmly to life.

Carla Stevens

TROUBLE FOR LUCY

Illustrated by
Ronald Himler

 Houghton Mifflin/Clarion Books/New York

Acknowledgments

Excerpts at the beginning of Chapters 1, 3, and 4, are from Peter H. Burnett's "Recollections of an Old Pioneer," *Oregon Historical Quarterly,* Volume 3, 1902.

Those beginning Chapters 2, 5, 6 and 7 are from Jesse Applegate's "A Day with the Cow Column in 1843," *Oregon Historical Quarterly,* December 1900.

Both Peter Burnett and Jesse Applegate were part of "The Great Migration of 1843." For a while, Mr. Burnett was captain of the first group of wagons. Mr. Applegate followed behind with the huge herd of cattle.

Library of Congress Cataloging in Publication Data

Stevens, Carla.   Trouble for Lucy.

"A Clarion Book."
Summary: As she and her family travel the Oregon Trail in 1843,
Lucy's puppy persists in creating trouble.
[1. Frontier and pioneer life—Fiction. 2. Oregon trail—Fiction.
3. Dogs—Fiction] I. Himler, Ronald. II. Title.
PZ7.S8435Tr   [Fic]   79-10445   ISBN 0-395-28971-8

Contents

Foreword 7

1 · Along the Trail 9

2 · More Trouble for Lucy 19

3 · Where Is Finn? 27

4 · Lost and Found 39

5 · Wagon All Alone 49

6 · A Friend Next Door 59

7 · One More Makes Four 67

Afterword 78

THE OREGON TRAIL

Foreword

Less than one hundred and fifty years ago, Oregon was not yet part of our country. At that time the territory was claimed by both the United States and Great Britain. Some believed that the best way to resolve the argument was to fill the land with American settlers.

The promise of free land was one reason why a group of emigrants—200 men, 130 women, and 610 children—left Independence, Missouri, in May of 1843 for Oregon. (An emigrant is someone who leaves one place to settle in another.) At first they traveled together in 122 covered wagons, along with almost 5,000 head of cattle. But they soon found the wagon train too long, so they divided in half.

In this story, Mr. and Mrs. Stewart and their daughter, Lucy, were among those who had no more than two or three cows. They went ahead as part of the first group of 61 wagons. The rest followed behind with the huge herd of cattle.

Some of the emigrants who traveled west kept diaries of their journey. Others wrote long letters to friends and relatives back home. Still others wrote reports and books after their journey had ended. You will read an excerpt from one of these accounts at the beginning of each chapter.

These valuable records have helped me to imagine what life might have been like for young Lucy Stewart in the first weeks of her long journey to Oregon in 1843.

Carla Stevens

1

Along the Trail

"The place where we encamped was very beautiful and no scene appeared to our enthusiastic visions more exquisite than the sight of so many wagons, tents, fires, cattle, and people as were here collected."

* * *

Lucy Stewart walked beside her farm wagon carrying a small fox terrier in her arms. Every few minutes she stopped and tried to shift the wriggling puppy from one arm to the other. She sighed as she gazed ahead at the vast expanse of sky. A thin layer of clouds veiled the sun, already low on the horizon.

"I'm so wore out, I just can't hold you another minute, Finn," Lucy said, as she leaned over to put the puppy down. "Now you behave, you hear?"

9

The black-and-white puppy squirmed out of her grasp and bounded ahead.

"Lucy!" Mr. Stewart's deep voice carried above the creaking of the wagon wheels. "Lucy! Get that dog away from here! How often do I have to tell you that he is not to go near the oxen!"

"Oh, no, not again." Lucy groaned. "Finn! Come here!" She lunged at the puppy but he was too fast for her.

"Miles!" she called, spying a tall, sandy-haired boy ahead. "Catch Finn!"

Miles turned just in time to block the puppy's path. He scooped him up in his arms.

Lucy ran toward them. "Oh, thank heavens, you got him, Miles. Whatever am I going to do with Finn?"

"I wouldn't worry," Miles said. "He'll learn to behave when he gets a little older."

A bugle sounded. Miles handed her the puppy and broke into a run. "I've got to help Pa. See you later."

"Break line!" came the call. Suddenly there was a mix of new sounds.

Lucy heard her father shout "Haw!" in his deep voice, the signal for the oxen to move to the right. One wagon after the other turned slowly inward to form a big circle.

As soon as their own wagon was in place, Mr. Stewart began unhitching the six oxen. Lucy put Finn down and ran to take the three heavy yokes, one by one, from her father and place them against the side of the wagon. Then Mr. Stewart hooked one end of an ox chain to a front wheel and the other to a wheel of the Abbott wagon alongside theirs. The wagons, linked together by the chains, formed a corral for their cow, Brownie, and for the other horses and mules.

"Lucy," her father called. "See that the chickens are let out. Then bring me a bucket."

Lucy looked around for Finn. For the moment he was off chasing a group of small boys. If only he will stay away until I finish my chores, she thought.

Lucy went to the rear of their wagon. Underneath, swinging from the axle, were two wooden cages. One held Rufus, their rooster,

11

and the other held three squawking hens. Lucy bent over and unlatched each of the cage doors. Rufus and the hens half flew and half jumped out onto the ground and began to peck at insects in the short grass.

Ma had already opened a large chest at the end of the wagon bed and was taking out the tin plates and the cups needed for supper. Lucy tried to ignore the strained look on her mother's face as she handed her a bucket.

"Here, Lucy," her mother said. "Give this to your father and I'll get the eggs."

Suddenly her mother stumbled in a tangle of puppy leaps and bounds. Lucy caught her just in time to keep her from falling.

"Oh, I'm so sorry, Ma!" She frowned at the little dog who was jumping up and down. "No, Finn! No!"

"It was my own fault, Lucy. I was just not looking where I was going." Mrs. Stewart bent down and tried to quiet Finn. "You'd better tie him up, Lucy. He'll be after the chickens again."

Lucy took a rope from inside the wagon and

tied Finn to the rear axle. The little black-and-white dog began to strain at the rope, barking and whining.

"Hush, Finn." Lucy bent down and gave him a quick pat. "Please, please hush. I'll be back soon to feed you."

Carrying the bucket, Lucy headed for the river. Each night she helped her father check their oxen's hooves for thistles, small stones, and grass stubble that might have become imbedded in them. Lucy knew how important it was to take good care of the oxen. They could never travel all the way to Oregon without them.

Lucy began scrubbing one of Sunny's hooves with soap and water when she heard her father shout, "Git! Git away, I tell you!"

She looked around and saw Finn bounding in and out of the oxen's legs. One end of the rope was around his neck, the rest was trailing behind him. Her heart sank.

"Lucy, I told you to keep that dog away from the oxen. Why do you persist in disobeying me?"

"But I tied him up, Pa," Lucy said. "I tied him

14

to the wagon tongue." She heard a yelp and turned to see Finn limping away from one of the oxen.

"What did I tell you!" her father said gruffly.

Before Lucy could reply, Miles ran forward and picked up Finn. "I'll take care of him until Lucy is through with her work, Mr. Stewart," he offered.

Thanking Miles with a small smile, Lucy knelt down and began to scrub again. Ever since they left Independence, Missouri, Pa had been so cross. Lucy knew it had to do with Ma. Ma was going to have a baby soon. The motion of the wagon made her feel sick. She could scarcely eat anything and every day she seemed to be getting weaker and weaker.

One night last spring Lucy had heard her parents talking. "I'll never forgive myself if anything happens to you, Abigail," her father had said. Lucy had wondered then what could happen. But that was before she knew her mother was going to have a baby.

Lucy glanced up and saw her father gazing down at her. She looked away quickly, afraid he might say something more about the puppy. Instead, he said quietly, "Run along now, Lucy, and see if you can find more fuel for the fire. I'll milk Brownie tonight."

"Yes, Pa." Lucy ran back to the wagons to look for Miles. She found him talking to Prudence Abbott. Prudence's long blond curls were partly hidden by a bonnet that framed her pretty face. The Abbotts were Quakers and came from a large town in Ohio. Even though they traveled right behind the Stewarts, Prudence was not very friendly. Well, that didn't bother Lucy one bit. Who would want to sit in a wagon all day knitting or reading the way Prudence did?

Miles was holding Finn in his arms.

Prudence touched the puppy gingerly. "See. He has only a bruise on his back leg. We checked him carefully all over."

Lucy reached out to pat Finn. He licked her dusty face.

"Oh, thee shouldn't let him do that," Prudence said. "My mother says dogs can make thee sick."

Prudence and her mother are even sillier than I

thought, Lucy said to herself. She looked at Miles. "You can put him down now, Miles. I'll tie him up and then I've got to go look for more buffalo chips."

"So do I," Miles said. "Do you want to come, Prudence?"

"Oh, no," Prudence replied. "My brothers have gathered all the wood we need."

How Lucy wished she had four older brothers! What a fuss they made over Prudence. Why she had no chores at all to do except help her mother with the cooking. Lucy glanced at Prudence's clean gray dress with its wide collar. Prudence wouldn't look nearly so perfect if she had to help tend to the oxen or milk the cows.

Lucy picked up the rope Finn was dragging and tied him securely to her wagon tongue. After tugging the rope to make sure it was fast, she gave Finn a bowl of buttermilk. Then she ran off to join Miles and the other children.

☙ 2 ❧

More Trouble for Lucy

"It is not eight o'clock when the first watch is to be set; the evening meal is over . . . Before a tent near the river a violin makes lively music, and some youths and maidens have improvised a dance upon the green; in another quarter a flute gives its mellow and melancholy notes to the still air."

* * *

Every evening it got to be a contest among the children to see who could collect the most buffalo chips. Miles had already found quite a few pieces of dried dung by the time Lucy caught up with him. She knew it was no use looking for any dead wood around the campground. It had been gathered and used by other travelers who had passed this way before.

By the time Lucy returned to her wagon, bits

of wood and buffalo chips were already burning in a small trench that Pa had dug. Each day as they traveled, Lucy and Pa picked up all the twigs and dead branches they could find along the trail and stored them in the wagon for their campfire. There was not enough flame from this fire to warm them on a cold night, but it was hot enough to cook the supper on their sheet-iron stove.

Lucy dumped her armful of chips on the ground nearby and sat down, exhausted. Ma looked up and smiled at her as she wiped the last bit of flour off her hands. Lucy guessed buttermilk biscuits were baking in the Dutch oven. The lamb's tongue and wild onions she herself had gathered along the way were frying in salt pork in the three-legged fry pan.

Pa had cut short sticks from the willow bushes along the river and was sharpening the ends with a knife. A week ago Ma had boiled some buffalo meat. When it cooled, Lucy helped her cut it into thin strips and hang it to dry inside the wagon. Now the jerky was ready to be roasted on the end of a stick.

On either side of them, people were chatting to one another as they ate around their campfires. Lucy could see Prudence passing out plates full of food to her brothers. Suddenly they all burst out laughing at something Prudence said. I wish we had something to laugh about, Lucy thought. She looked at her mother, who sat staring at the little fire, her food still untouched on her plate. Lucy felt she must say something.

"I heard we come eighteen miles today," she tried.

Pa just grunted. Lucy could tell he was tired. The swarms of mosquitoes buzzing around them were making him even more cross. He swatted at them furiously.

Suddenly, Finn appeared. He snatched a piece of jerky from the wooden trencher lying beside the fire.

Mr. Stewart jumped up. "Lucy, this is the last straw!" he said angrily, "that puppy must go."

"Now, now, Will, it's all right." Lucy's mother reached up and tried to pat her husband's arm. "He's only a puppy. He'll learn to behave."

"You know I was against taking that puppy along. Your brother had no right to give him to Lucy without asking me first."

"But Uncle John meant no harm, Pa," Lucy protested. "He thought Finn would be good company for me along the way."

"John never had an ounce of sense and he never will," Lucy's father said.

"Will, how can you say that about my own brother?" Mrs. Stewart said quietly.

"I will not have my daughter disobey me," Mr. Stewart went on, ignoring his wife's remark. "You told me you tied him up, Lucy."

"But I did, Pa. I really did." Lucy stepped on the rope trailing behind Finn and picked him up, hugging him close. She struggled to hold back her tears. "Oh, Finn, how did you ever get loose again?" She carried the puppy to the wagon and put him inside.

Later that evening, after the supper dishes were cleaned and Lucy had caged Rufus and the hens, she climbed into their wagon, taking care not to bump the lighted lantern that hung from the center bow. Finn was sound asleep on her bed.

She took off her dress and hung it on one of the hooks that were fastened to the six hickory bows supporting the canvas top. Then she lay down on the bed, covering herself with a blanket. From outside, she could hear people laughing and talking. How different life was here! At home on the farm, their closest neighbor lived almost eight miles away. On the wagon train people were everywhere. It must be like living in a busy town, Lucy thought. It would be fun having someone my own age right next door. Not Prudence Abbott, though. I could never be friends with her.

Lucy could hear her father hammering his tent stakes nearby. Oh, if only Ma were well and Pa were not so cross all the time.

"Lucy?" Mrs. Stewart lifted the hem of her long skirt and climbed awkwardly into the wagon. She sat down next to Lucy and began removing the pins that held her two long braids

in a coil around each ear. "Don't mind your pa, child. He's worried about me. But Dr. Whitman paid me a visit day before yesterday. He will tend me when my time comes." She kissed Lucy, blew out the lantern, and lay down beside her. "I'll be just fine, I know it."

"Of course you will, Ma. And tomorrow I'll see that Finn stays out of Pa's way." Soon her mother's steady breathing told Lucy that Ma had fallen asleep.

Usually Lucy felt so snug inside their little house on wheels that she promptly fell asleep too. But tonight she lay awake for a long, long time thinking. For the first time she realized how much Pa disliked Finn. It was not just because he was a frisky puppy. It had something to do with Uncle John.

She remembered the harsh words that were exchanged between Uncle John and her father before they left Ohio. Uncle John did not think Ma was strong enough to travel all the way to Oregon. What if Uncle John were right?

How she wished she could do something to

make Ma feel better. But she knew there was nothing anyone could do now but wait for the new baby to be born.

Where is Finn?

"The white-sheeted wagons and the fine teams moving in the wilderness of the green prairie made the most lovely appearance."

* * *

Lucy snuggled down in her bed, pulling the blanket tight around her. Something had awakened her. Surely it was not the crack, crack of rifles? It was still so dark in the wagon.

She listened. Yes, there was the sound again. She could hear her father moving around outside. Four o'clock, time to get up. She rolled over to look at her mother lying beside her and saw that she, too, was awake.

"How do you feel, Ma?" Lucy asked.

Her mother sighed. "I can tell," she said, patting her large belly. "It won't be long now."

"Lucy! Lucy!" Her father was calling her.

"Hurry now. Brownie needs milking."

"Coming, Pa," Lucy called. She sat up and reached for her dress. No time to brush and rebraid my hair, she thought.

"Your father expects too much of you, Lucy dear," her mother said.

Lucy leaned over and gave her mother a kiss. "That's all right, Ma," she said. "I can do it."

She finished dressing quickly, then jumped out of the wagon, taking a small stool with her. Finn stood in the wagon looking down at her, the rope still tied around his neck. He wagged his tail hopefully.

"No, Finn. You stay right there until I come back."

Lucy shivered slightly. The early morning air felt damp and heavy. It was still dark, though a faint gray light began to appear in the east. Pa came toward her out of the darkness, leading a cow. He tied the cow to the back of the wagon. Lucy sat on the stool and wiped Brownie's udder with a clean cloth before she began to milk her.

The rich, warm liquid squirted into the pail with a hissing sound as Lucy squeezed first one teat, then another. When she finished, she leaned her head against the warm side of the friendly brown-and-white animal.

A feeling of homesickness swept over Lucy. She closed her eyes and thought about that spring morning back in Ohio when the dew on the fields sparkled like millions of jewels. She had been the first to find the newborn lambs in the big, musty barn. There were not one, but two—twins—born to her favorite ewe, Amelda.

Lucy opened her eyes. It was no use thinking about Ohio. They were never going back, Pa said. They had nothing to go back to. Their farm had been sold. Six hundred and forty acres of free land were waiting for Pa to claim in Oregon, plus 160 more for Ma and 160 more for each child.

After covering the milk pail, Lucy carried it to the wagon and put it inside. Then she led Brownie over to join several other cows grazing nearby in the corral. Brownie traveled with a small herd of cows and horses watched over by Miles's oldest brother.

Pa had the breakfast fire started by the time Lucy got back. Once again, the two of them ate in silence.

"I'll take some coffee to Ma," Lucy offered.

"No," her father said. "She's not hungry this morning."

After the fire was put out and the cooking utensils washed and stored again, Pa rounded up their oxen and drove them into the corral. Lucy picked up the first yoke that had been leaning against the wagon side, walked to the end of the wagon tongue, and waited.

Following Pa's commands, the oxen lumbered slowly to the wagon and stood in position alongside the tongue, waiting to be yoked. After Pa had yoked the three pairs of oxen, he fastened one to the other with a long chain. Way ahead, Lucy could hear a faint "Catch up! Catch up!" Then, "Giddap! Giddap!" until it was her father's turn to move. The wagon train was rolling again.

Lucy looked up at the low gray clouds blanketing the sky. She tossed a handful of cracked corn to Rufus and the hens in their cages beneath the wagon. Then she climbed inside the wagon and took the cover off the milk pail. She carefully poured the cream that had risen to the top of the pail into the butter churn. By nighttime the cream would be churned into butter by the motion of the wagon.

Lucy half expected Finn to be looking out at her.

"Finn!" she called. Her mother's breathing was slow and steady. She had fallen asleep again. Lucy looked around carefully, but Finn was not there. "Oh, Finn!" she whispered. Then she started feeling for the lumps Finn usually made under her blanket on the bed. But there were none. "Oh, Finn," she repeated, "please don't cause more trouble for me today."

Lucy backed out of the wagon. Without thinking, she ran up to her father, who was walking alongside the oxen. "Pa, have you seen Finn?" she asked. The look on her father's face made her sorry she had asked.

"I have not," he said. "Don't tell me that dog is loose again!"

Lucy began to run before her father finished

speaking. She couldn't bear to hear what he might say to her next. The wagons stretched out ahead in a long line. Except for an occasional "Giddap!", no one talked much. It was in the early morning when both people and oxen were rested that they made their best time.

"Finn! Here, Finn!" Lucy's high voice caused heads to turn in her direction.

"Hey, little lassie! Keep running like that and you'll be all wore out by noon," someone said.

A huge Irish wolfhound began loping behind Lucy until its master called, "Moira! Here!"

"Have you seen my dog, Mr. Burnett?" Lucy asked, as she passed the captain of the wagon train walking beside his oxen.

"Don't know what yours looks like, Lucy," Mr. Burnett replied. "So many dogs running about."

Lucy silently counted the wagons as she ran. Ten, eleven, twelve, then two more—at last she reached the Chapin wagons. She spotted Miles walking with his father.

"Miles!" she said breathlessly. "Oh, Miles,

I've called and called and I can't find Finn anywhere."

"I'll help you look." Miles turned to his father. "May I, Pa?"

Mr. Chapin nodded.

Lucy and Miles moved from one wagon to the next, calling and asking until they reached the lead wagon. Then they turned back, checking again. But no one had seen a little terrier puppy.

"Maybe Prudence will help us look," Miles suggested. "She really likes Finn."

"She may like Finn but I don't much like her," Lucy said shortly.

"I think we should ask. At least Prudence knows Finn." Miles persisted.

Lucy glanced at Miles. He really likes Prudence, she thought. When they reached her wagon, Lucy was afraid Pa would ask her about Finn. But he stared straight ahead, hardly aware that she and Miles had passed him.

They found Prudence sitting in the wagon seat beside her mother. Lucy looked at her and felt a twinge of envy. Her dress was so neat, her bon-

net in place. Even Prudence's shoes were not dusty and dirty like Lucy's old brogans. Lucy touched her sunburnt nose. I guess it pays to wear a bonnet, she thought.

"Good morning, Lucy," Mrs. Abbott said. "How is thy mother today?"

"She is still asleep," Lucy answered.

"It is good that she can rest," Mrs. Abbott said.

"Prudence, have you seen Finn?" Miles asked.

"No, Miles. Is he lost?"

"He isn't lost," Lucy said stiffly. "We just can't find him. Come on, Miles. Let's head toward the rear of the wagon train. Maybe he's running along with all the other dogs."

Miles turned. "See you later, Prudence."

"I hope you find Finn, Lucy," Prudence said.

Lucy felt like saying, "If you really cared about Finn you'd get down off that seat and help us look for him." But she didn't.

Lucy and Miles stopped at each wagon to ask if anyone had seen a little black–and–white puppy.

36

When they reached the rear of the wagon train they saw many dogs but not Finn. Lucy was trying to hold back her tears.

"Oh, Miles, do you suppose he got left back at the campground?"

"No chance of that," Miles replied quickly. "Don't you know how carefully they check the grounds before the wagon train moves on? Nothing ever gets left behind."

"But they could miss a little puppy, Miles," Lucy said.

"No, I'm sure not," Miles said firmly. "Someone would have seen him."

"But what if they didn't see him? What then?" Tears began to roll down Lucy's cheeks. She wiped them away quickly and hesitated for a moment, looking at Miles. Then she began to run.

"Wait, Lucy!" Miles called, running after her. "Where are you going?" He grabbed her arm.

"Let go, Miles. I'm going back to the campground and check to be sure."

"But Lucy, you can't do that!"

Lucy faced her friend. "Yes, I can. Ma is

asleep. I'm not needed until noon. No one will miss me until then. And by that time I'll be back."

"But it's going to rain." Miles looked up at the heavy gray clouds moving swiftly across the sky.

"Promise not to tell, Miles," she said in a low voice.

"Do I have to promise?" Miles asked.

"Yes. Promise."

"Well, all right," Miles said. "But what will I say if you don't come back?"

"I'll be back. If anything bad happens to me, I can always wait for the second wagon train to pass." Lucy touched Miles's arm. "Don't worry."

She turned and began running again. In just a few minutes she had left Miles far behind.

4

Lost and Found

"We here saw a band of Pawnee Indians return-
ing from a buffalo hunt. They had quantities of
dried buffalo meat, of which they generously gave
us a good supply."

* * *

Raising a cloud of dust, a small herd of cattle, horses, and mules followed behind the last
wagon. Lucy skirted the edge of the herd and ran
along close to the river, hoping no one would see
her. They could not have traveled more than a
mile or two from the campground. It would be
so easy to get there and back before anyone
noticed that she was missing.

When she was far enough behind, Lucy left the
riverbank and returned to the trail. A damp, cool
wind began to blow against her back, pushing
her along faster. She shivered slightly. Across

the river in the distance, she could see slowly moving brown and yellow spots. She knew they were antelope and buffalo grazing in the low rolling hills beyond. They never came near their wagon train like the wolves. Sometimes at night she could hear them howling. Ever since she saw how wolves had dug up a shallow grave, she had been afraid to look closely at the mounds marked by a simple stone or cross along the trail.

She passed a prairie dog town. One little animal sat up straight watching her until she came very close to his burrow. Then he gave a funny high bark and disappeared into his hole. Finn wasn't much bigger than you are when Uncle John gave him to me, Lucy thought.

The wind blew harder. Lucy stopped for a moment and looked back at the wagon train. Far across the prairie she could still see the wagons, though now they too looked like specks. The sky to the west was heavy with black clouds. Was that a drop of rain? She began to run again, forcing herself to go faster. The trail broadened. Ahead, she could see the campground—a wide area of hard-packed earth and grass trampled by wagons, people, and animals. "Finn!" she called. "Here, Finn! Here, Finn!"

She felt a sharp sting. Then another and another. Hailstones! A clap of thunder rolled overhead. Now the hailstones began falling faster and faster, bouncing off her head and shoulders. They fell so fast that the ground was soon covered with the small, round ice balls.

Lucy ran toward the river and crawled under the first willow bush she saw. Crouching down, she covered her head with her arms to protect herself from the pelting hailstones. What if the storm got worse? What if it didn't stop all day? Her stomach was in a tight knot and tears began to roll down her cheeks.

"I can't stay here," she whispered. "I must start back." Water was running down her face, her neck—her braids were soaking wet. She lifted her head. Oh, please God, let me find Finn. "Finn! Finn!" She screamed his name. Until this moment she had never once doubted she would find her puppy. But now she was not so certain. Perhaps when he discovered that the wagon train had left, he had run in the other direction. Per-

41

haps he had spotted an antelope and begun to chase it. Or perhaps. Perhaps Pa had—Oh, no, Pa wouldn't do anything to Finn without telling her first. "Finn," she sobbed. "Please, Finn. Answer me!"

Was that a bark? Or just the noisy rumble of the hailstones? Again she called the puppy's name. She listened and heard something. It was an animal sound, she was sure of that. Lucy crawled out from under a bush and began to move toward the sound. "Finn! Here, Finn!"

A real bark answered her call. Ahead, she saw something moving slightly under a gooseberry bush. Could it be? Oh yes, yes. It *was* Finn!

When he saw Lucy, he began barking and wagging his tail. "Oh, Finn. What happened to you?" Lucy was half sobbing and half laughing as she bent over him. The thorns on the gooseberry branches scratched her hands when she tried to pick him up. But the rope was wound round and round the bush holding him fast. She hugged and kissed the wet squirming puppy and he licked her face and her ears.

Lucy untied the rope around Finn's neck and then unwound it from the bush. The hailstones had begun to turn into rain. Here and there big hailstones that had not yet melted rolled like marbles under the soles of her shoes. I must get started back this minute, she thought. It will not be easy to catch up when the ground is so muddy.

She began to follow the ruts made by the wagon wheels through the wet prairie grass. Finn bounded along joyfully beside her. The rain was turning into a drizzle. Ahead, toward the west, she saw a patch of blue sky appear through the clouds. But the wagon train was not in sight. What will Pa do to me if he finds out? Lucy tried to push away the bad thoughts she had had about Pa just before she found Finn.

Lucy stopped suddenly and listened. She could hear a muffled sound in the distance. Thunder perhaps, she decided. But no, the sound was steady and growing louder by the minute. It was coming from her right across the river. Looking in that direction, she saw a group of people on horseback riding toward her. Her heart jumped.

They cannot be from the wagon train. Were they Indians?

She began to run faster along the trail, stumbling as she watched the horses coming closer and closer. Now they were fording the river. Yes, they were Indians. She could see the brown-and-white markings on their ponies. She thought of hiding along the riverbank until they passed. "Finn!" she called in a low voice. But just then Finn saw the ponies and began to bark wildly. It was no use. They would surely see the puppy even if she did hide. She could feel her heart pounding in her ears.

"Finn! Come here!" she said sharply. The puppy ran to her. She picked him up and held him tight as she watched the ponies gallop toward her. There were five men. She could see haunches of buffalo slung over the backs of several ponies. They must be returning from a hunt, she thought.

Laughing and talking among themselves in a strange language, the men halted their ponies in a semicircle around Lucy. One young man, who wore deerskin leggings and a topcoat over a calico shirt, spoke directly to her. Lucy noticed that his black hair was cut short, not shaved like the Indians she had seen in Independence. She felt his dark eyes piercing through her. Shaking her head, she said, "I can't understand you."

The man turned to the others and they began talking among themselves again. They must be saying something about me, Lucy thought. Oh, if only I knew how to speak to them! I could explain why I am here. I could say that I belong to the wagon train far ahead, that I really must be moving on or I will never, never be able to catch up.

She held up Finn and pointed back toward the campground. Then she pointed ahead. The Indians turned but there was nothing to be seen on the horizon. Lucy tried again. She pointed to the tracks made by the wagon wheels, then to the west. "My wagon train is over there," she said.

Lucy was beginning to feel chilled. Her wet clothes clung to her body. She took a few steps. When she walked, her water-soaked shoes made a squishing sound. It's no use, she thought, her

eyes filling with tears. I will never be able to catch up now.

For the first time, the man in the topcoat smiled down at her. Uttering a few words, he leaned toward her and held out his hand, then gently patted the place in front of him on his horse. Now he was pointing at Finn.

For a moment Lucy hesitated. Then she stood on tiptoe and held Finn out to him. "Here," she said. Why, he could hold Finn in one hand!

The young man smiled and leaned down, extending his other hand and speaking softly to her again. Once more Lucy hesitated as she looked up at him.

"I want to go home," she pleaded. "Please, please take me home."

She held her arms out to him and felt herself being pulled onto the horse. As soon as she was astride, the man handed her the puppy. His strong right arm now held her firmly on the saddle blanket.

Signaling to the others to follow, the young man turned his horse and began galloping toward the west.

5

Wagon All Alone

"An emigrant's wife . . . is now taken with violent illness, the doctor has had the wagon driven out of line, a tent pitched and a fire kindled."

* * *

At first the horses followed the trail along the South Platte River, but they soon veered away from the river and cut across the wide prairie. Lucy had thought they were heading in the right direction. Now that she could no longer see the river, she was not so sure.

The wind blew through Lucy's wet clothes. She tried to keep her teeth from chattering and held Finn tightly so that his fat little body could warm her. But she began shivering violently. All of a sudden, the young man drew in the reins until his horse stopped. He jumped off and then on again. This time he sat in front of her and held Finn.

"Oh, thank you!" Lucy huddled against the man's back, holding tightly to his coat. She was out of the wind now and was feeling less cold.

They galloped on and on, faster than she had ever galloped before. She remembered Red Cloud, their good friend in Ohio, telling her how swift Indian ponies were—much faster than their horse, Star. Red Cloud was an Algonquian who spoke English well because he had lived around white men all his life.

These young men might be Pawnees. Pa had told her that ten years ago more than half the Pawnees had died from a disease called smallpox,

caught from the white men. The Pawnees who
survived did not often come near the wagon
trains traveling through their territory.

Suddenly Lucy saw a line of black ants on the
horizon. She laughed, knowing that they
weren't really ants at all.

"Look!" she pointed ahead. "There's the
wagon train!"

Far ahead, Lucy saw someone on horseback. Is
he coming to look for me? she wondered uneas-
ily. But the man did not approach them. Instead
he passed by, far to the north.

They continued to gallop toward the wagon train until they reached the herd of cattle and horses.

"Hey, Lucy!" shouted Miles's brother. "What are you doing up there?"

She waved. "I'll tell you later," she called back.

Lucy began to shiver again, and this time she knew she was trembling with anxiety. What would Pa do when he found out where she had been? She must get off this horse before they reached her wagon. She tugged at the man's coat and pointed to the ground. But he only nodded.

They continued to ride past wagon after wagon. As Lucy passed the Abbotts, she caught a glimpse of Prudence sitting in the front seat staring at her in astonishment. Ahead was her own wagon. She tugged at the man's coat again, this time much harder. The Indian slowed down his horse just as Lucy spied Miles walking beside her oxen.

"Miles!" she called out. "I found Finn!"

Miles stared at the Indians. His eyes grew big and round.

"Where is Pa, Miles?" she asked.

"He's gone to get Dr. Whitman for your ma," Miles said. "He couldn't find you so he left me in charge."

Lucy had forgotten all about Ma. She felt sick with fear. Was that Pa she had seen riding so fast across the prairie? She pulled at the Indian's coat sleeve. "I want to get down," she pleaded. "Please, please let me down."

The young man turned and looked at her questioningly. Then he reined his horse to a halt. Lucy half slid, half jumped off the horse's back. She reached up and took Finn from the man.

Mrs. Burnett and another woman were walking behind her wagon. Lucy squeezed in front of them and tried to look inside. She could see Mrs. Abbott but not her mother.

"I want to see Ma," Lucy said.

"Soon, child," Mrs. Abbott replied softly. "But not now. Thy mother is very busy. Thee must run along."

"But I'm wet," Lucy said in a small voice. "I need dry stockings."

"Ask Prudence to give thee a change of clothes," Mrs. Abbott said. Then she pulled the puckering string so that the canvas closed tight. Lucy could no longer look inside.

Lucy didn't want to see Prudence. She wanted to see her ma. She walked around to the front of the wagon to find Miles. He was so excited when he saw her again that he hopped up and down.

"Weren't you scared, Lucy?" he asked. "I mean about those Indians. I heard a story once about how they stole a girl and took her to their village to live."

"I was scared when I first saw them because they were strangers," Lucy said honestly.

"You have all the luck. I sure would like to ride on an Indian pony."

"Where did they go, Miles?" Lucy asked.

"The Indians? They rode up front to see their friend, John Gantt. He can speak Pawnee, you know."

"I didn't even thank them for helping me. I would never have caught up with the wagon train if they hadn't found me."

Just then they heard galloping horses behind them. Lucy and Miles turned to see two men on horseback riding fast toward the wagon train.

Miles pointed at them. "That's your father and Dr. Whitman."

Lucy put Finn down and watched her father drawing closer and closer. What shall I tell him about Finn? she wondered. She looked at her damp dress and muddy shoes. He'll be so angry with me.

But her father scarcely paid any attention to her. After he and Dr. Whitman dismounted, he handed her the reins.

"Take off Star's bridle, Lucy. See that he joins the other horses," he said.

Lucy watched her father follow Dr. Whitman to their wagon. Mrs. Abbott stepped out and then Dr. Whitman climbed inside.

Star stamped and snorted impatiently while Lucy unfastened the bridle. As soon as she took it off, he galloped toward the herd of cattle and horses.

Suddenly Lucy heard a low moan come from

inside the wagon. She had never heard a sound quite like it before. It took her a second to realize that it was Ma who had made that strange sound. There is was again—another long, low moan.

Dr. Whitman leaned out of the wagon and said something to her father. Mr. Stewart quickly went up to Miles and, without a word, took the whip out of his hand.

"Gee, Boss. Gee!" her father called to the oxen. The oxen obeyed and turned to the right, pulling the wagon out of the line.

"What is happening?" Lucy asked.

"You go along with the wagon train, Lucy," her father said grimly, taking the bridle from her. "We'll follow later."

"But I want to stay with you!" Lucy's eyes filled with tears.

"Do as I tell you!" Her father turned away, busying himself with the oxen.

"Lucy, go and see Prudence." Mrs. Abbott gently patted her shoulder. "She is waiting for thee."

One after another, the wagons rolled onward.

"Come along, Lucy," someone called as he passed her.

Lucy turned one last time and stared through her tears at the wagon standing alone on the prairie. She heard Ma call out, "Will! Oh, Will!"

6

A Friend Next Door

"The wagons form a line three-quarters of a mile in length; some of the teamsters ride upon the front of their wagons, some walk beside their teams; scattered along the line, companies of women and children are taking exercise on foot. They gather bouquets of rare and beautiful flowers that line the way."

* * *

Lucy walked alongside the moving wagons trying to push away anxious thoughts about her mother. Lots of mothers had babies. Didn't Ma say she would be fine? But Ma was having a baby in a covered wagon far out in the prairie. And she sounded as if she were afraid and in pain. Lucy wished Pa had let her stay with him. It was so much worse not knowing what was happening.

"Lucy! Lucy!" Lucy turned and saw Prudence

coming toward her leading Finn on a rope. "Lucy, I brought thee Finn."

Prudence Abbott is the last person I want to talk to now, Lucy thought. "Thanks," she said curtly. She took the rope and kept walking, hoping that Prudence would go away.

"My mother says thee is to come to my wagon and get a change of clothes," Prudence said.

Lucy looked at Prudence, prim and proper as usual. I don't want to go with you, she said to herself. I don't want to be with someone I don't like when I've got things to think about.

Mrs. Burnett leaned out of her wagon. "Lucy, you really must go with Prudence and change into dry clothes before you catch cold."

"Yes, Mrs. Burnett." Lucy looked down at her muddy shoes and wet stockings. I must look pretty awful, she thought. But I don't care a bit.

Lucy followed Prudence to her wagon. Prudence climbed inside first. "Here," she said reaching out. "Give me Finn."

Lucy handed her the puppy and climbed in behind her. The inside of the wagon was so much like hers that she felt as if she were home.

Prudence took a gray linsey-woolsey dress off one of the clothing hooks. "Put this on, Lucy."

"I don't want to wear your dress," Lucy said. "I'm not that wet."

"But thy shoes and stockings are." Prudence pulled out a pair of heavy stockings from a chest. "At least put these on."

Lucy took off her wet stockings and put on the pair that Prudence had given her.

"I'm so glad thee found Finn." Prudence sat down on the bed beside Lucy and patted Finn. "I wish my mother and father would let me have a dog, but they don't believe a child should have a pet."

"Oh," Lucy said. As if she cared about what Prudence could or couldn't have!

"Lucy . . . " Suddenly Prudence leaned toward her and spoke almost in a whisper. "I have a confession to make to thee."

Lucy looked at Prudence in surprise. "A confession? What kind of a confession?"

"Well, yesterday I was the one who untied Finn."

"You did! Why did you do that?"

"He was whining and barking, and once he got all tangled up in his rope. I thought thee was mean to keep him tied—so I untied him." Her words seemed to tumble out.

"That was a bad thing to do," Lucy said. "You got me in a lot of trouble."

"Miles told me about all that," Prudence said. "I'm sorry."

"You should be," Lucy said sharply.

"But Lucy, I didn't do anything to Finn today. I never even saw Finn. Thee must believe me. Oh, please don't be angry with me," Prudence begged. "I'm telling thee the truth."

"If someone didn't untie him, then he must have fallen out of the wagon," Lucy said. "He probably tried to follow me to the river and the rope he was dragging got caught on a bush. No one heard or saw him in all the confusion of leaving."

"Oh, I'm sure that's what happened, Lucy," Prudence said.

"At least you could have helped us look this morning," Lucy said. "You just sat there."

"Oh, I wanted to. But my mother and father don't approve of the—well, the rowdy children on the wagon train."

Lucy frowned. "So I'm one of those rowdy children."

"I didn't mean thee, Lucy. My mother likes thee, really she does. She just expects me to be different, that's all."

I've had enough of Prudence, Lucy thought. She is prim and prissy—and mean besides.

"They expect me to be perfect," Prudence went on. "And my brothers too. Lucy, thee doesn't know how lonely I am."

Lucy almost laughed out loud. "Prudence, how can you be lonely with four brothers? Every time I see you you've got someone making a fuss over you."

"But I *am* lonely." Prudence twisted her fingers together. "I want a friend my own age. Someone I can talk to. Like thee."

"Me?" Lucy laughed in spite of herself. "Oh, no. We are too different, Prudence. Why, I

64

would die of boredom if I had to sit in a wagon all day like you."

Prudence looked as if Lucy had slapped her face. "I guess thee is right," she said softly. "I'll let thee rest a while." She got up from the bed and moved to the front of the wagon.

I've hurt her feelings, Lucy thought. I didn't mean to say that.

"Prudence, you can play with Finn any time you like," Lucy offered. "That is, if my father lets me keep him."

Prudence turned and looked at Lucy in alarm. "Oh, surely he will let thee keep him!"

"I'm not so sure. My pa is very strict. And he's going to be very angry with me when he finds out what I did today."

"But I will tell him I am to blame for what happened yesterday," Prudence said. "Then he will know it was not thy fault."

"I don't think it will matter," Lucy said. "He's cross with me most of the time lately."

"My mother says that is because he is so concerned about thy mother."

"I know that." Lucy hesitated. "Listen, Prudence. I'm sorry about what I just said. I didn't really mean that we couldn't be friends. There are lots of things we can do together. After all, we live right next door."

Lucy suddenly felt exhausted. She lay back on the bed and closed her eyes for a moment. Sometime I will tell Prudence how lonely I feel, she thought to herself. Lucy opened her eyes, then closed them again. The motion of the wagon was making her feel so sleepy. . . . In another moment, she was fast asleep.

7

One More Makes Four

". . . as the sun rolls down, the absent wagon rolls into camp, the bright speaking face and cheery look of the doctor, who rides in advance, declares without words that all is well and both mother and child are comfortable."

* * *

When Lucy woke up, the wagon had stopped. She had no idea how long she had slept.

She scrambled to the front of the wagon and pulled back the canvas flaps. The smell of campfires filled the air. All the wagons were already chained together in a circle for the night. She saw Prudence and Mr. and Mrs. Abbott bending over their fire. Finn was tied to a wagon wheel. But where were Ma and Pa?

Lucy put on her shoes and jumped down from the wagon. Mrs. Abbott looked up and smiled.

"Has my wagon come yet?" Lucy asked timidly.

"No, my child," Mrs. Abbott replied. "But thee'll see. It will be along very soon."

A young boy leading a cow passed by and she suddenly remembered Brownie.

"Pa will be mad at me if I forget to milk our cow."

"Prudence will bring thee a pail and a stool," Mrs. Abbott said.

"I don't think they have herded the animals into the corral yet, Lucy," Mr. Abbott said. "There isn't enough grass in the circle to keep them content all night."

A group of horses and cows were grazing on the prairie to her left. Lucy thought she could see Brownie munching grass alongside their horse, Star.

Just as she reached the herd, she saw a man coming toward her on horseback. When she recognized Dr. Whitman she ran toward him, waving the pail as a signal for him to stop.

"Please, sir, how is my mother?" she called out.

Dr. Whitman drew his horse to a halt. "Are you the Stewart child?" he asked.

Lucy nodded.

"Your mother is very well indeed. And you, my dear, have a baby sister."

A baby sister! Lucy turned and ran back to the Abbotts. "Prudence! Prudence! Mrs. Abbott! I have a baby sister!"

"Oh, Lucy, I'm so happy for you," Prudence said.

Mrs. Abbott smiled. "Dr. Marcus Whitman is a fine doctor. I knew everything would be all right."

Lucy felt an urge to jump up and down, but the milk pail kept banging against her leg.

"I almost forgot to milk Brownie again. Pa would not be pleased." She ran back and got the cow and tied her to the rear of the Abbott wagon.

"Congratulations, Lucy!" Mr. Burnett passed her, leading a horse.

"Thank you," Lucy replied, surprised that he already had heard about the new baby.

"Lucy!" Miles was running toward her, holding out two fish. "I heard the news! Hey, look at the two big catfish I caught! There are loads more in the river. You just got to come fishing with me after supper."

"I can't, Miles," Lucy said. "I'm waiting for Ma and Pa to come." Why, he's more excited about those fish than my new baby sister, she thought.

"Your wagon is coming but it's still only a speck in the distance."

Lucy's heart gave a jump.

"Gee, you look funny, Lucy. What's the matter?" Miles asked.

"Nothing, Miles," she said. She sat on the stool and placed the pail on the ground under Brownie's udder.

"What about the Indians?" Miles asked. "Are you going to tell your pa about Finn and the Indians?"

Lucy didn't answer. She bent her head, leaning closer to the cow as she milked.

"Maybe your pa won't find out," Miles went on. "Then you won't get in any more trouble."

"I don't know what to do, Miles," Lucy said soberly as she stood up. "If Pa finds out what I did, he probably won't let me keep Finn." She handed Miles the pail of milk. "Here. Take this to the Abbotts while I attend to Brownie for the night."

She unfastened a chain that extended between two wagons and gave the cow a friendly slap on the rump, heading her into the corral. She was still thinking about what Miles had said as she refastened the chain. Maybe if she didn't say anything, Pa would never find out about Finn. Maybe the Pawnees would be gone by the time Pa got back. But down deep, she knew better than to believe that. There were no secrets on a wagon train.

Lucy looked out over the prairie. The white canvas top of the approaching wagon looked like a small ship sailing before the wind. Suddenly, more than anything in the world, she wanted to see Ma and the baby. She began to run. What did it matter about what Pa would do to her? What mattered was that Ma was well and that she had a new baby sister.

She was almost out of breath when she heard her father call to her. "Lucy!" His deep voice rang out across the prairie. "Lucy, child! You have a sister!"

"I know, Pa! I know!"

Pa looked at Lucy and laughed for the first time in two months, a deep rolling laugh. "And thank God, your mother is just fine. Go and see her now, child."

Lucy ran past her father and the oxen to the back of the wagon and climbed inside. Her mother was lying in bed. Beside her was a little white bundle.

"Oh, Lucy. Dear, dear Lucy. I'm so very glad to see you."

Lucy crawled forward on the bed. Her mother reached out and drew her close. Lucy lay there feeling warm and safe. The bundle moved just a little and Mrs. Stewart parted the blanket. Yes, it was a baby all right, but oh, it was so tiny. Lucy looked at the little fingers and the tuft of black hair on her head and the funny, red, squeezed-in face.

"She looks just the way you did when you

were born, Lucy dear," her mother said.

The wagon stopped.

"Congratulations!" Mrs. Abbott was peering into the wagon. "I know thee needs rest, Abigail, but I've made thee a custard."

"Thank you, Sara," Mrs. Stewart said. "I feel fine, just fine. I expect to be up and around in the morning after a visit from that good Dr. Whitman. Do come and see the baby. She is beautiful."

"Lucy!" Mr. Stewart's voice boomed through the canvas. "Lucy! I want to speak to you."

Lucy jumped. Pa knows. Why did he have to find out so soon?

"Dear, you look as if you have just seen a ghost," said her mother. "What's the matter?"

"Nothing, Ma. It's nothing." Lucy kissed her mother and gave the little blanket a pat before she climbed out of the wagon. Lucy saw Mr. Burnett walking away from her father. Pa's back was to her. When he turned, he was not smiling.

"Why didn't you tell me you couldn't find Finn?" he asked in a low voice.

Lucy looked down at her shoes. "I thought

you would be glad he was gone," she said softly.
"He was causing so much trouble."

"Oh, Lucy, Lucy."

Something in her father's voice made Lucy
look up at him.

"What would I ever do if I lost you?" he said.
Suddenly he picked her up and held her tight.
Lucy buried her face in his shoulder. "I'm sorry,
Pa," she whispered. "I'm so sorry."

"You must promise me never to go away
from the wagon train by yourself again. It is
very, very dangerous. I hate to think what might
have happened to you . . ."

"I promise," Lucy said.

"You and Ma and the baby are the whole
world to me. Don't you know that, Lucy?"

"Yes, Pa."

Her father held her out away from him and
looked at her soberly. "Now Lucy, your mother
mustn't hear about this for a while. It would
upset her so. She thought you were visiting a
neighbor when the storm came."

Mr. Stewart put her down almost as abruptly
as he had picked her up. "I have much to be

thankful for today. Now I must go and see the men who brought you here safely. Mr. Burnett tells me they know Captain Gantt well and have offered a good supply of buffalo meat to the wagon train."

"Pa?" Lucy touched her father's arm timidly.

"Yes, Lucy."

"Pa, may I keep Finn? I'll see that he stays out of your way. Prudence and Miles will help me, too."

Mr. Stewart looked down at his daughter and nodded. "Finn is your dog, Lucy."

"Oh, thank you, Pa!"

Lucy turned and saw Prudence, with Finn in her arms, waiting for her.

"Prudence!" she called. "Pa says I may keep Finn! Just think! We'll have a puppy and a baby to play with all the way to Oregon!"

Afterword

On the 16th of October, 1843, the Stewart family arrived in Fort Walla Walla, Oregon. Peter Burnett figured out that they had traveled 1,600 miles from Independence, Missouri.

This trip became known as "The Great Migration." Many more people traveled to Oregon in the years following, but "The Great Migration" was the most important because it proved that travel by wagon was possible. By 1846 so many settlers were in the territory that Great Britain was forced to give up her claim to the land. Oregon became part of the United States at last.

For many emigrants, the journey west by wagon was the most exciting event of their lives. They loved the company, the new sights, the adventure. It is true that travel by wagon was not easy. There were many hardships along the way, especially when they reached the Wind River Mountains. But on the whole, the emigrants were as healthy as those who remained at home. In later years a disease called cholera caused many deaths on the wagon trains. But many people also died from an epidemic of cholera in the cities back east.

Everyone remembers hearing stories about bands of American Indians galloping out of the hills to attack a wagon train. But no emigrant's diary or journal tells of such an attack. We know now that these stories simply are not true.

Native Americans were not a serious concern to the emigrants until the 1860s. By that time Native Americans were beginning to realize what was happening to them. The white men were killing off the buffalo and the other animals they depended upon for food. They were keeping the best land for themselves and giving the worst to the Indians. Native Americans began to fight much more fiercely to defend the land that was rightfully theirs. But it was too late. They were outnumbered. By 1890 more than 100,000 men, women, and children had traveled 2,000 miles across America to settle in the west.

About the Author

Carla Stevens was born in New York City and received her B.A. and M.A. degrees from New York University. Formerly an editor of children's books at a New York publishing house, she now conducts writing workshops at the New School for Social Research. Other Clarion books by Ms. Stevens are *Pig and the Blue Flag, Hooray for Pig,* and *Stories from a Snowy Meadow.*

About the Illustrator

Ronald Himler was born in Cleveland, Ohio, and now lives in New York City with his wife and two children. He studied painting at the Cleveland Institute of Art and after a wide variety of occupations, began illustrating children's books. So far he has illustrated thirty books for children, and has written three. *Trouble for Lucy* is his first book for Clarion.